The Haunted Museum

One night the Director was working late in his office when suddenly he knew that he was no longer alone. The figure of a young woman in a long cloak, with a scarf covering her hair, was sitting across from him. She looked as pale as death. Indeed, her form seemed to be almost transparent.

"What do you want?" he whispered.

The figure stood up. There was a ghostly smile on her face. She let the cloak fall from her shoulders. The body under the cloak was that of a corpse. It was half-rotted. Over the heart there was a huge gaping wound. The museum Director was so horrified he was unable to move. Slowly the figure faded away . . .

T ◇ H ◇ E
RESTLESS DEAD
Ghostly Tales From
A R O U N D
The World

DANIEL COHEN

*Illustrated with photographs,
prints, and drawings*

AN ARCHWAY PAPERBACK
Published by POCKET BOOKS • NEW YORK

Pictures on pages 6, 16–17, 38–39, 50, 53, 59, 78–79, 82–83, 93 and 96 from New York Public Library Picture Collection; drawings on pages 25, 31, 42, 62, 71 and 88 by Arthur Thompson

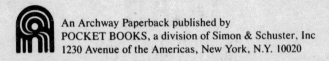

An Archway Paperback published by
POCKET BOOKS, a division of Simon & Schuster, Inc
1230 Avenue of the Americas, New York, N.Y. 10020

Copyright © 1984 by Daniel Cohen
Cover artwork copyright © 1987 Terry Oakes

Published by arrangement with Dodd, Mead & Company
Library of Congress Catalog Card Number: 83-24447

ISBN: 0-671-64373-8

First Archway Paperback printing October 1987

10 9 8 7 6 5 4 3 2 1

AN ARCHWAY PAPERBACK and colophon are
registered trademarks of Simon & Schuster, Inc.

Printed in the U.S.A.

IL 4+

For Carol

CONTENTS

INTRODUCTION

IT'S THE SAME THE WHOLE WORLD OVER

Perhaps you have heard of "friendly ghosts" or "helpful spirits." I'll bet you don't believe in any of those things. I certainly don't. Most of the people in the world don't believe in "friendly ghosts" either.

People from Canada to China, from Australia to Italy know this: If you meet something from beyond the grave the best thing to do is get out of its way—fast! Because it probably isn't going to be very friendly at all.

We are going to look at a group of stories that illustrate this point. They come from all around the world and from different periods in history. They are stories about ghosts, and other spirits of death, about walking (and riding) corpses, poltergeists, even haunted furniture.

Are any of these stories true? Not a single one of them would stand up in a court of law. None can be used as scientific proof of the existence of ghosts or anything else. They are simply stories—the sort of stories that people have always told to one another late at night.

I can't claim that any of these stories really happened as they are told. But at midnight, when there is a storm outside, and the wind rattles a branch up against your window, every one of these tales will seem quite true enough.

Enjoy them—just as people all over the world have enjoyed ghost stories for centuries.

1

THE MUMMY'S GHOST

There have been many, many terrifying tales inspired by the mummies of Egypt. But this one is unusual. It is set in the German city of Dresden in 1894.

Herr Frederick Wiser was the Director of the Egyptian department at the Dresden museum. One day he received a strange letter. It came from a man named Schultze. Herr Schultze was offering to sell the museum the mummy of an ancient Egyptian princess. The name of the princess was Nitokris. She was well known to history, but her mummy had never been found. Now Schultze said he had the mummy in his house in Dresden. He invited the Director to come over and examine the mummy anytime he wished.

Normally, Wiser would have thrown such a letter in the wastebasket. Museums receive a lot of crank mail. But as it happened, he knew Herr Schultze. Schultze was a small-time dealer in antiquities. The museum had bought some items from him in the past. In his dealings with Schultze, the Director had always found him most satisfactory.

Wiser passed the letter on to his assistant, Karl Bruch. "What do you think of this?"

Bruch read the letter and said, "The man must be mad. How could he get such a valuable and famous mummy without the whole world knowing about it?"

"I'm sure you are right," answered the Director. "Yet we have had some good things from this man. And sometimes very valuable and unusual items do turn up in the oddest places. You know there is a huge trade in illegal Egyptian items. We will have to be very careful. But it is worth a look. Schultze does not live very far from here."

Bruch was doubtful. But he agreed to go with the Director to Schultze's house where the mummy was supposed to be kept.

The house was in a run-down section of Dresden. The prospect of finding something of value in such a place did not seem very promising.

The Director knocked at the door several times. There was no answer. Just as the Director and his assistant were about to leave, the door opened. An old man—tall, stooping, and shabbily dressed—came to greet them. It was Herr Schultze.

"Please come in, gentlemen," he said.

He led them up a flight of stairs to the parlor. The furniture was old and worn. There was nothing to suggest that this was the home of a man who possessed a priceless mummy.

The Director felt very uncomfortable. "I received your letter this morning, Herr Schultze," he said.

"My letter, yes. You are interested in the Princess Nitokris?"

"Frankly, we find it hard to believe that so valuable a mummy could exist without the knowledge of museum authorities."

"It is strange, I agree," said Schultze. "But there are many strange things in this world."

The Director was annoyed by Schultze's vagueness. "Our time is limited, Herr Schultze. Perhaps we could see the mummy."

"Of course. I will be happy to show her to you."

Schultze led the Director and his assistant to a small locked storeroom. In the center of the room was an Egyptian coffin. It seemed to be a coffin of late Egyptian times, the time of Princess Nitokris. The Director examined the coffin in the dim light. It seemed real enough.

"May we see the mummy?" he asked.

"Certainly," said Schultze. He lifted the coffin lid. Inside lay a small figure tightly wrapped in linen. The linen had become brown with age.

The museum Director had seen Egyptian mummies before.

Carefully the Director examined the markings on the wrappings. They bore the name of Princess Nitokris.

"Beautiful, isn't she?" said Schultze. "You have nothing like her in your collection at the museum."

The Director tried not to show his own eagerness. Such a find would be a feather in the cap of the Dresden museum. It would make him the envy of museum directors all over the world.

"We will have to examine this more closely, at the museum," he said.

"Of course, of course," said Schultze. "You will find her perfect."

"And naturally we will have to know more about how this mummy came into your possession."

Schultze's voice became hard. "I can tell you nothing of where she came from. I have sworn to that. I can only tell you that the mummy is mine to dispose of as I wish."

"You have no objection if we check with the police?"

"Do what you like," said Schultze.

The following day the mummy was taken to the museum. As far as anyone could tell, the coffin was genuine. The police could find no record of the theft of a mummy. But there were still many, many unanswered questions. However, the Director wanted this exhibit for his museum at all costs. So he brushed aside any questions. And he paid Schultze the huge sum of money he had asked for.

The mummy was put on display immediately. It proved to be the popular attraction that the Director had hoped it would be.

About a week after the mummy was put on display, Director Wiser was working late in his office. As he started to leave, he was stopped by one of the women who cleaned up in the museum at night.

"Oh, sir," she said, "there is a young woman in the Egyptian gallery."

"Nonsense," said the Director. "All the visitors have gone home hours ago. Are you sure you didn't see one of the other cleaning women?"

"No, sir. This was a very young woman. She was wrapped in a cloak and had a scarf around her head. There was something very strange about the way she moved. Her feet didn't seem to touch the ground. She didn't make any sound."

"My employees are seeing ghosts in the Egyptian gallery," thought the Director. "I had better do something before the rumor spreads."

Wiser and the cleaning woman searched the gallery. They talked to the other cleaning people, and to the night watchman. No one had seen anything. Wiser then told the cleaning woman that she had been the victim of some sort of an illusion. Museums at night were spooky places. Museum workers sometimes saw things. Why, he sometimes saw things himself. Actually, he didn't, but he wanted to reassure the woman. The cleaning lady left, a bit ashamed of herself.

Two days later the night watchman reported seeing a similar figure. The Director talked the matter over with his assistant, Bruch. The night watchman had worked in the museum for years. He was an old soldier. He was not the sort to be "seeing things." They decided that he must have been talking to the cleaning woman and believed her story. The Director and his assistant agreed that it would be best to ignore the whole thing.

That's what they did. And no strange sights were seen for a week. But then the figure appeared again. This time Bruch himself saw it.

He was sitting in his office. Slowly he became aware of a presence. He was no longer alone. He looked up and saw the figure of a woman standing by the wall. She was standing in the shadows and Bruch could not see her clearly. He had the impression of a young woman wearing a long cloak, with a scarf over her head.

"Who are you?" he cried. "What do you want?" Instantly the figure vanished.

The museum Director was beginning to believe that his whole staff had gone crazy. But

A page from the Egyptian *Book of the Dead*

there was more to come. Visitors to the museum began seeing the ghostly figure in the Egyptian gallery near the mummy of Nitokris.

The Director seriously began to wonder if the museum was being haunted by the ghost of the long-dead princess of Egypt. If so, it was a very odd haunting. The figure that people saw was not a mummy. It was not wrapped in linen bandages. The figure wore a modern cloak, and had a modern scarf covering her head.

Still, the museum Director could not bring himself to believe that anything out of the ordinary was happening. "People will soon get tired of this, and our ghost will disappear forever," he told himself.

And sure enough, for a while the figure did seem to disappear. A whole week went by and no one reported seeing it.

Then, as he often did, the Director was working late in his office when suddenly he knew that he was no longer alone. The figure of a young woman in a long cloak, with a scarf covering her hair, was sitting across from him. She looked as pale as death. Indeed, her form seemed to be almost transparent.

"What do you want?" he whispered.

The figure stood up. There was a ghostly smile on her face. She let the cloak fall from her shoulders. The body under the cloak was that of a corpse. It was half-rotted. But that was not the worst. Over the heart there was a huge gaping wound. The figure removed the scarf around her head. This revealed another deep wound.

The museum Director was so horrified he was unable to move. Slowly the figure faded away. Only after it disappeared entirely was he able to move again.

What he had seen was not the phantom of some long-dead Egyptian princess. It was the ghostly corpse of a recently murdered young woman.

The next morning the wrappings were removed from the mummy. They covered the corpse that the Director had seen. The corpse had been partly embalmed, and then wrapped to look like a mummy.

When the police visited Schultze's house, they found that he had already left. It seems that he, too, had seen the figure in the Egyptian gallery, and knew what it meant. In his house they found all the tools of the forger. Schultze was very good at his dishonest craft. He had started by selling small fakes. Then he decided to fake something really important, like a royal mummy.

Several months later the forger was picked up in Prague. He was still trying to sell forged ancient objects. He quickly admitted the murder of the young woman, but would give no details.

"She was nothing," he said. "I made a royal princess of Egypt out of nothing. I could have made kings and emperors."

Schultze had gone completely mad. It made no difference. They hanged him for murder anyway.

2

THE WOMAN IN WHITE

This story comes from Japan. Two woodcutters were on their way home late one evening. One of the woodcutters, Mosaku, was an old man. The other, Minokichi, his assistant, was eighteen years old.

The weather was very cold, and it started to snow. The woodcutters had to cross a wide river before they reached their village. There was no bridge on the river. The only way to get across was by using a small ferryboat. When Mosaku and Minokichi reached the river, they found the boatman had gone for the night. He had tied his boat on the other side of the river.

The woodcutters could not cross the river that night. They decided to take shelter in the ferryman's hut. There was no heat. Still, the two thought themselves lucky just to be out of the wind on such a night. The storm was growing worse by the moment.

Old Mosaku fell asleep quickly. Minokichi was cold and uncomfortable. He lay on the

The "snow ghost" is one of the many spirits of winter in Japanese folklore.

十九

floor of the hut listening to the wind howling. Finally, he also fell asleep.

Suddenly, Minokichi was awakened by a blast of icy air. Someone had opened the door to the hut. The snow was blowing in his face.

Then he became aware of the figure of a woman standing in the room. The woman was dressed all in white. She was leaning over the old man, breathing on him. Her frozen breath looked like white smoke.

The woman then turned to Minokichi. He tried to get up, but he could not move. He tried to scream, but was unable to make a sound. The woman leaned closer and closer to him. Minokichi could see that she was very beautiful. But there was something about her eyes that terrified him.

The woman stopped, and looked at Minokichi. She smiled and then she said softly:

"I was going to kill you. Just like I killed the old man. But you are very young. And you are very handsome. I feel sorry for you. I am going to let you live. But if you ever say a word about what you have seen tonight—to anyone, even you own mother—I will know. Then I will kill you. Remember what I say."

The woman turned, walked through the doorway, and disappeared into the snow. As soon as she was gone, Minokichi found he was able to move again. He rushed to the door, but could not see the woman. Nor could he find any footprints in the snow. He began to think it had all been a dream. He went over to Mosaku to tell the old man about his dream. The old man did not move. He was cold and dead. It had been no dream.

The storm let up by morning. When the boatman came to his hut, he found Minokichi unconscious next to the frozen corpse of the old man.

It took Minokichi a long time to recover from that terrible night. But he did not forget the warning that the woman in white had given him. He did not say anything about what he had seen—or thought he had seen—that night.

After a few months Minokichi went back to his job of woodcutter. Every morning he went out into the forest. Every evening he made his way back to his village. One winter evening, about a year after the night in the boatman's hut, Minokichi met a girl on the road. She was tall, slim, and very good looking.

Since they were both going in the same direction, Minokichi and the girl started talking. She told him that her name was O-Yuki. She was a poor orphan, and she was looking for a job as a servant. The more they walked, the more charmed Minokichi became. He asked O-Yuki if she was married, or had any plans to be married. She replied no.

By the time they reached the village, Minokichi had made up his mind that this was the girl that he wanted to marry. He took O-Yuki to his house to meet his widowed mother. She was also charmed by the young woman. And so, as things turned out, O-Yuki never went any farther looking for a servant's job. She remained in Minokichi's house and became his wife.

She was a very good wife. When Minokichi's mother died five years later, her last words were praise of her daughter-in-law.

As the years went by, O-Yuki bore Minokichi ten children, five boys and five girls. They were all unusually tall and strong, and all very light like their mother.

At first, the people of the village were suspicious of O-Yuki. They were country people and suspicious of all strangers. Finally, they came to accept her, even to admire her. Still, they knew she was different. In the village, life was hard. After a woman had a few children she aged. She began to look like an old woman. But O-Yuki had ten children and had not aged at all. She looked just the same as she had the day she entered the village for the first time.

One night, after the children had gone to sleep, O-Yuki was sewing by lamplight. Her husband looked at her. For the first time he noticed something.

"You know," he said, "seeing you there in the lamplight reminds me of something that happened to me a long time ago. It was before I met you. I was only eighteen."

Without lifting her eyes from her sewing, O-Yuki said, "Oh, tell me about what happened."

Minokichi then told her about the terrible night in the hut. He told her about the woman in white who had bent over him, smiling and whispering.

"As I remember her, she looked very much like you do now," he said. "Of course, it was a long time ago, and it may all have been a dream."

O-Yuki threw down her sewing. She rushed over to where Minokichi sat, leaned over him, and shrieked in his face:

"It was I! And I told you that I would kill you if you ever said one word about it to anyone. If it were not for those children asleep in there, I would kill you this moment. Now you had better take very good care of them. If they ever have reason to complain about you, I will know about it, and I will treat you as you deserve."

As she screamed, her voice faded off into a howl, like the wind. And she melted away to a white mist that disappeared through the chimney.

She was never seen again.

3

A Ride for a Corpse

In Turkey they tell this ghostly little tale.

There was a young man who set out on a long trip on horseback. The trip was to take him through country that was unknown to him.

The trip turned out to be longer and more difficult than he had expected. By the third day he was already well behind the schedule he had set for himself. Then he was delayed practically the entire day on business.

In order to make up for some of the lost time, the young man decided that he would have to ride through the night. He knew a night ride would be difficult. But he was strong and vigorous. He had ridden all night before.

He started out just before sunset. It was almost completely dark when the young man found himself passing a cemetery. There, sitting on a stone by the side of the road, was a girl of about sixteen or seventeen. She was crying.

The young horseman could not pass by so

sad and appealing a figure. He stopped to ask her what was wrong.

The girl sobbed out a story of how she had to get to a distant town by the next morning. But she was already so tired that she could not possibly make the trip—particularly at night.

The young man, feeling very gallant, offered to take her.

"My journey takes me past that very town," he said. "My horse is strong and fresh. He can carry both of us."

Tearfully, the girl thanked him.

He hoisted her up to the saddle, and climbed up behind her, so that he could hold her. He grasped the girl firmly by the waist and spurred his horse. The horse galloped off with a surprising burst of speed.

They rode through the night. The young man's horse, instead of tiring and slowing down, seemed to go faster and faster. It was almost as if the horse was driven by some unknown but powerful terror. When the young man tried to reign his horse in to slow it, he was not able to do so.

Something even stranger was happening. The girl riding in front of him did not say a word, though he tried to talk to her several times. As he clung to the girl, she seemed to grow heavier, and harder to hold. At first the young man thought this was his imagination. Perhaps he was becoming weary, and she just seemed heav-

The horse was driven by some unknown terror.

ier. But as the night wore on, the change in weight became unmistakable. After a few hours he felt as if his arms would fall off. Yet he couldn't let go, even if he wanted to.

As dawn was breaking, the riders reached the town to which the girl had wanted to go. The horse stopped suddenly on its own. It stood frothing, and trembling with exhaustion. The young man too was trembling, but from fear more than exhaustion. He was able to loosen his grip on the girl. She tumbled from the horse and sprawled on the ground—a lifeless corpse.

A small number of early risers in the village witnessed the scene. They did not seem the least surprised. The young man was afraid that they would accuse him of killing the girl. He told them he had no idea what had happened. He said that the girl had been alive and well when he picked her up. Somehow, she had died during the trip.

But the villagers were quick to assure him that he would not be accused of any wrongdoing. This same thing had been happening for years, they said. They told him a strange story. The girl had died ten years ago. But the family had decided to bury her in a cemetery far from her native village. Every year, on the anniversary of her death, she tried to return to her native village in this way.

Don't worry, they told him, the girl's relatives would be along shortly to take the corpse back to its distant resting place—for another year anyway.

The young man continued the rest of his trip during daylight hours only.

Don't be surprised if this story sounds familiar to you. It is very like the tale of the phantom hitchhiker—the most popular and widespread of all American ghost legends. That is the story of a young man who is driving along a deserted road at night. He stops to pick up a young girl who is hitchhiking. When he gets to his destination, he finds that the girl, whom he thought had been asleep in the back seat, has vanished. Later, he discovers that the girl had been killed ten years earlier in an auto accident at the very spot at which he had picked her up. On the anniversary of her death she always tried to hitchhike home.

Obviously neither story is "true"—but they are always told as if they are. No one seems to know which version of this tale is the original, or if the stories are really related to one another at all.

4

The Amherst Mystery

Poltergeist—it's a German word. It means noisy spirit.

When a house has a poltergeist, objects are thrown around. There are strange noises, raps, and thumps. Sometimes something will be broken. These happenings generally center around a young person. Reports of poltergeists are fairly common. Most of the time nothing really awful happens. After a while the poltergeist just goes away.

But sometimes poltergeists can be dangerous. One of the best-known cases of a really nasty and dangerous poltergeist comes from Canada. It began in the small city of Amherst in Nova Scotia, in 1878.

The location for these weird, and sometimes terrifying, events seemed ordinary enough. It was a plain two-story cottage. The cottage had been rented to Daniel Tweed, a shoe factory foreman. Tweed lived there with his wife Olive, and two very young sons, George and William.

Also living in the house were two of Olive's sisters, Jeannie and Esther. Jeannie was twenty-one. Esther, around whom the events centered, was nineteen.

As with most poltergeist cases, the Amherst affair started rather quietly. One night in September, Esther jumped out of bed screaming. She said she thought there was a mouse in the bed. Esther and Jeannie searched the room but found nothing.

The next night Esther and Jeannie were awakened again. They heard noises coming from a box under the bed. They thought the mouse had been caught. But when they took the box out from under the bed, the box began jumping around the room all by itself. There was no mouse in the box.

A day and a night went by and nothing happened. The strange events were almost forgotten. In the evening Esther said that she wasn't feeling well. She went to bed very early. About ten o'clock she woke up screaming. Her face and arms had swollen up horribly. "What's the matter with me?" she cried. "I must be dying."

While Esther was still crying out, there was a tremendous bang heard throughout the house. The family rushed around to see if anything had been broken. Nothing seemed to have been touched. The source of the noise could not be found.

The activity centered around the girl, Esther.

After a few hours Esther's swelling went down. She returned to normal. She fell asleep immediately. The house was quiet and peaceful for the rest of the night, and for the next four days and nights. Then it began again.

The covers were suddenly and mysteriously ripped off Esther's bed. Tweed put them back on again, and they were immediately pulled off again. Pillows were thrown around the room. And poor Esther began to swell up again.

Tweed knew he needed help. He called in the local physician, Dr. Carritte. At first the doctor laughed at Tweed's story of strange noises and flying pillows. But it was obvious to the doctor that something was wrong with Esther.

As the doctor began to examine Esther, her pillow began moving around. The doctor tried to hold it still, but he couldn't. The room was filled with knocking and scratching sounds. No one could tell where the sounds were coming from.

Then they realized that the scratching represented the poltergeist's attempt to communicate. They watched as these words were scratched on the wall: "Esther Cox, You Are Mine to Kill."

The knocks and rappings continued for another two hours. At one time they got so loud that they knocked some of the plaster out of the wall. Dr. Carritte wasn't laughing anymore. He agreed to return the next day.

When he came back, the doctor accompanied Esther around the house. At one point the poltergeist threw potatoes at both of them. Dr. Carritte also heard what he described as "sledgehammer-like poundings" throughout the house. That was enough for him. He left and didn't come back again.

The strange happenings in the Tweed house began to attract the attention of other citizens of Amherst. Every morning a crowd gathered around the house. Finally, the crowd grew so large that the police had to be brought in to control it.

Esther now became very ill. She was unable to get out of bed for weeks. After she began to get a bit better she was sent to another sister's house to recover. During this whole period the poltergeist did nothing.

Now you may think it was all Esther's fault, that she was throwing things around, and making the noises. That's what a lot of people thought, and that's what a lot of people said. There is no doubt that all of the strange happenings centered around nineteen-year-old Esther. But many witnesses swore that she could not have created the disturbances herself. They saw Esther sitting on one side of the room, while there were sounds coming from the other side. They said they saw objects thrown at her.

They said that there was no way that Esther could have done what the poltergeist did.

When Esther finally returned to the Tweed house she brought the poltergeist back with her. Now the poltergeist had a new trick. It began playing with lighted matches. Esther insisted that she could hear the thing talking to her. It was saying that it was going to burn the house down. Lighted matches began falling, apparently from nowhere. Small fires were started all over the house. Tweed managed to put them out but he was badly shaken.

Esther's sister Jeannie also began to say that she could communicate with the spirit. She said the spirit's name was Bob, and that Bob did indeed intend to burn down the house. There were more small fires.

Tweed did the only thing he could think of. He threw Esther out of the house. She got a job in a local restaurant, but the disturbances followed her. Chairs and tables in the restaurant were mysteriously knocked over. Very soon Esther was out of a job. Tweed took her back.

About this time a showman named Walter Hubbell came to Amherst. He thought there might be a way to make some money off the poltergeist. He would put Esther on the stage. He said people would pay to see the poltergeist mysteriously move objects around. The poltergeist, however, did not cooperate. Esther sat on the stage, but nothing happened. The great money-making scheme fell flat. The customers demanded their money back.

Tweed finally had enough of Esther and her troublesome spirit. He threw her out of the house once and for all.

The rest of Esther's life seems to have been an unhappy one. She wandered from place to place. At one point she was accused of burning down her employer's barn. She said the poltergeist did it. The judge didn't believe that story, so Esther Cox spent some time in jail. She claimed that her life had been ruined by the poltergeist.

What are we to make of such a tale? Was Esther Cox a faker? Was she crazy, so that she didn't know what she was doing? Or was she pursued by some sort of angry, invisible spirit that did ruin her life?

5

THE DUST

For centuries the island of Malta in the Mediterranean had been a major port for the British navy. The island always had pleasant associations for Lieutenant March. Always, that is, until that one strange experience. Now the Lieutenant insists that he would never return to Malta again—not even if his life depended on it.

Here is what happened—or what Lieutenant March thinks happened. The Lieutenant and a fellow officer, Lieutenant Andrews, had dinner at the house of one of Malta's leading citizens. The dinner had been an extremely pleasant one. The hours sped by. When the two officers left it was very late.

The good food, good wine, and good talk had put the men in an excellent mood. But the lateness of the hour made them hurry a bit.

March stopped at the entrance to a narrow street. "I think if we go up here, we can reach the harbor more quickly. This street should be a shortcut."

The harbor at Malta

"Right," said Andrews. And so the two men turned into the dark and narrow side street.

It was a street of private homes. Everybody seemed to be asleep. There were no lights in any of the windows. The street itself had only a few feeble streetlights. The officers had no feelings of fear. The streets of Malta were safe. And all streets led to the harbor. There was no chance of getting lost.

They had come about halfway down the street when they saw a figure standing by one of the houses. As they got closer they saw it was a woman. She seemed to be in some trouble. She was trying to open a window of one of the houses, but without any success.

"We had better see if we can help," said March. Andrews nodded in agreement.

As the two officers got closer, they saw that the house was one of the largest on the street. It had an elaborately carved front door. The woman herself was dressed very formally. She wore a long black dress which nearly swept the ground. Atop her head and trailing down to cover the lower part of her face was a Spanish-style black lace veil called a *mantilla*. Her manner of dress was the sort that would have been popular with the wealthier Spanish women of the island.

"Can we be of any help, madam?" asked Lieutenant March.

"Oh, thank you," she said. She spoke perfect English, but her voice had a definite Spanish accent. "I am very embarrassed. I went out without taking my keys. All my servants are off attending a wedding feast in a distant town. They will not be back for hours. I found this small window unlatched. But it is stuck, and I am not strong enough to open it."

March stepped up and grasped the window. It took some effort, but he finally managed to pry it open. He climbed through the window into the house. The lights had been left burning in the hall. The woman's keys lay in plain sight on a table. March unlocked the front door and opened it.

The woman was extremely grateful. She invited Lieutenant March and his companion to stay for a drink. They protested that it was very late, and that they did not wish to intrude. The woman in the black dress insisted. She had the sort of personality that could not be easily opposed.

"I'm sure that officers of His Majesty's Navy will not reject a lady's invitation."

They did not.

As Lieutenant March began to look around the house, he was quite surprised. From the outside the house had seemed large. From the inside it seemed to be almost a mansion. The

"Rising up from the center of the hall was an elaborate double staircase."

hall had a floor of black-and-white marble. Rising up from the center of the hall was an elaborate double staircase.

The woman led the two officers up the stairs. These too were made of black-and-white marble. The men were taken into a small room at the top of the stairs. The room had only a few pieces of furniture in it. But the officers were able to see that these were fine and expensive antiques. This was the house of very wealthy people.

"Please make yourselves comfortable," the woman said. "I will go and get the drinks."

She returned in a moment with a silver tray. On the tray was a beautiful cut-glass decanter and three glasses.

The woman filled the glasses. Then she proposed a toast. "To your very good health, gentlemen."

"And to yours, Señora—ah—Señora . . ." said Lieutenant March. The woman ignored March's obvious request for her name. Yet she was not unfriendly. On the contrary, the two officers and the unknown woman chatted in a friendly manner for nearly half an hour. The officers then rose to leave, and the woman showed them the way down the stairs. They said their good-byes, and March held out his hand for a parting handshake. The woman did not respond. In fact, she stepped away.

After the two officers were out of the house

and back on the street, Andrews said, "That was very odd, wasn't it?"

"Odd in what way?" asked March.

"In lots of ways," responded Andrews. "She wouldn't tell us her name. She practically jumped when you tried to shake her hand. How did she get out of the house in the first place if it was all locked up, and the key was inside. And the house just sounded funny."

"Funny?"

"Yes, the way our voices echoed. There were drapes and carpets, but our voices and footsteps echoed just as if we were in an empty house."

"It was all a bit strange," March admitted. "But it's very late, and we have drunk quite a bit of wine."

The next afternoon the two officers were having lunch with an official of the island. Lieutenant Andrews was still puzzled by the events of the previous evening. He told the official what had happened. The official seemed confused by the tale. He asked Andrews to describe the house, and its location, again. He did, and Lieutenant March agreed that the description was absolutely accurate.

"What you have told me happened could not possibly have happened," said the official firmly. "I know the house you are speaking of.

It has been empty for nearly twenty years now. It has become little more than a ruin today."

"But we can't have been mistaken," insisted March. "The two of us remember the whole thing perfectly."

"I tell you that the house has been abandoned ever since Señora Suarez killed herself there. Her family was so grief-stricken that they could no longer enter it. They allowed the house with so many unhappy memories to go to ruin. If you can spare an hour I'll show you. Perhaps you were at a different house."

March and Andrews agreed to go with the official. As they approached the street, they had a growing sense of uneasiness. When they got about halfway down the street the official stopped and pointed. "Is that the house you say you entered last night?"

The carved front door was unmistakable. March and Andrews agreed that this was the house. They also realized that the official had been quite correct. The house was abandoned and falling into ruin. The door was weatherbeaten and riddled with worm holes. The window through which March had climbed was boarded up. So were many of the other windows in the house. And those that were not boarded up had been broken.

"This is impossible," insisted March. "Perhaps we were mistaken about the house. We must look inside." He pressed up against the door. It was locked, but the wood was so badly rotted that it split around the lock and the door swung open.

There was the black-and-white marble floor. And there was the elaborate double staircase. But now the walls were cracked, and everything was covered with a thick layer of dust.

Suddenly the official gasped, and stammered. "Gentlemen, I apologize for doubting you. Someone has been here very recently. Look!" He pointed to the floor. There in the dust were three sets of footprints, the prints of two men and a woman. Lieutenant March put his foot into one of the prints. The fit was perfect.

Silently, fearfully, they followed the prints up the stairs into the small room. Their footsteps echoed up the stairs just as they had the night before.

All the furniture in the room was gone except for the table that both March and Andrews remembered. In the dust that covered the table were the marks of three glasses.

The men stared at the table. Suddenly there was a violent draft. The dust rose in a thick swirling cloud that blinded them and choked them. Then, as suddenly as it started, the wind was gone. As they cleared the dust from their eyes, the men looked around. At first it seemed as if nothing had been disturbed. Even the layer of dust that covered everything looked as it had before. Well, not exactly as it had before. Where there had been the prints of two men and a woman, only the prints of the two men remained. And there were the marks of only two glasses in the dust on the table top.

March began to shake uncontrollably. "I'm getting out of here," he shouted. And he ran down the stairs, with the other two men right behind him.

After that, Lieutenant March wouldn't go back to Malta ever again.

6

THE DEMON CORPSE

In China an unburied body was once thought to be very dangerous. When a person dies, the spirit leaves the body. The body is then like an unoccupied house. Anyone, or in this case anything, might take possession of it.

The Chinese believed that the air was filled with invisible spirits and demons. One of these might take possession of any unattended corpse. The corpse could then be brought back to a sort of life. but it would no longer be the person who had previously inhabited the body. It would then be a creature called a *Ch'iang Shich*. That was an awful-looking thing with glowing eyes, long dagger-like nails, and a greenish skin. The breath of such a monster is deadly.

There is an old story about four travelers. They stopped at a roadside inn and asked for a place to sleep. But the inn was completely full. The travelers had come a long way and were

A demon ghost of China

very tired. It was starting to rain. The travelers begged the innkeeper to let them sleep some place, any place. Finally the innkeeper said there was a shed out back that they might sleep in. It wasn't very comfortable, but it was a roof over their heads. What the innkeeper did not tell the four travelers was that his daughter-in-law had just died. Her body was in the shed. It was stretched out on a plank behind a curtain. When the travelers entered the shed they didn't see the corpse.

Three of the travelers fell asleep at once. The fourth was uneasy, nervous. He couldn't get to sleep. He knew something was wrong. He just didn't know what it was.

As you might expect, the corpse had been invaded by a demon. It had become a *Ch'iang Shich.*

When the corpse thought that the travelers were asleep it got up. It carefully peered out from behind the curtains. The fourth traveler, the one who could not sleep, saw the bony hand draw back the curtains. He was too frightened by the sight to move. He just lay there, pretending to be asleep.

The creature leaned over each one of the sleeping travelers. As it did, it breathed on them. They died without waking up. When it approached the one traveler who had not fallen asleep, he kept his eyes tightly shut, and held his breath. That saved his life.

The corpse then returned to its place behind the curtain. When the surviving traveler thought it was safe, he jumped up and ran toward the door. But he made too much noise. The corpse heard him and chased after him.

The fleeing man could see the eyes of the creature glowing in the darkness behind him. He knew it was catching up to him.

He ducked behind a large tree to try and hide from it. He peered carefully around the tree to see if it was gone. It wasn't. He found himself looking directly into its glowing eyes. The thing was no more than three feet away. It let out a horrible shriek and jumped at him. He collapsed in a dead faint. That saved his life again. When he fell, the corpse missed him. It plunged forward with such force that it buried its long nails in the trunk of the tree. It was stuck.

The next morning when the innkeeper went to the shed to see about the travelers, he found the three dead men. He guessed what had happened. Then he went looking for the fourth man. He found the man unconscious on the ground near the tree. The corpse was there too—now truly and completely dead. Its long nails were still stuck in the tree.

A story, first told in China about 250 years ago, tells of a similar, but even more fearful, creature. This thing was supposed to have haunted a Buddhist temple. The creature was

A Buddhist temple and burial place

so awful that the temple was deserted at night. No one had ever actually seen the thing in the temple. They only heard it. They were too frightened to stay around and find out what it looked like.

One evening a shepherd asked permission to sleep in the temple. He wanted to stay close to his sheep which were under the temple porch. The priest warned him that something awful might happen. But the shepherd went in anyway. He was a very brave man and he carried only a candle and a whip.

Because of all the awful things he had been told about the temple, the shepherd was not able to sleep. Around midnight he heard noises. They seemed to be coming from beneath one of the temple statues. He lighted his candle. In the dim light he could see a gigantic figure with great claws and a greenish skin. Its breath smelled like a rotting corpse.

The monster attacked, but the shepherd was very quick. He managed to evade the claws. The shepherd struck at the thing with his whip. It didn't seem to feel the blows. It just kept coming after him. So the shepherd fled from the temple, leaving his sheep behind.

When it became light the shepherd went back to the temple. It was empty. But there was a strange and evil-smelling mist drifting from the cracked stone floor near some of the statues. It was at the spot where the shepherd had first seen the creature.

Digging, or in any other way disrupting a temple, was a very serious offense in China. The shepherd had to ask the local judge for permission. When he told the judge what he had seen, and why he wanted to dig up the stone floor, permission was granted at once.

When the stones were removed, the diggers found the mummified corpse of a gigantic man. The corpse fitted the description that had been given by the shepherd. The priest said that the only way to get rid of such a monster was to burn it.

A large fire was built. The giant corpse was thrown onto it. As the corpse crackled and burned in the fire it screamed and thrashed about. But soon there was nothing left but ashes.

The temple was never troubled again.

7

The Deadly Dinner

William Seabrook was an American writer. He spent a lot of time on the island of Haiti. He became fascinated by the practice of voodoo, and by tales of zombies, the walking dead. Seabrook told a lot of strange stories about Haiti. This is one of them. It isn't quite a ghost story, but when you finish I think you will agree that it's close enough.

The story is about a young girl named Camille. Her family, which had once been wealthy, had fallen on hard times. But Camille was a beautiful girl. Everyone in her family hoped that she would marry a wealthy man.

Because of her beauty and charm she quickly became one of the most popular girls in Port-au-Prince society. Port-au-Prince is Haiti's largest city.

As her family expected, she soon attracted the attention of a wealthy man. His name was Matthieu Toussel. He owned a large and prosperous coffee plantation in the mountains.

Toussel was a rather mysterious fellow. He had been born quite poor, but made a lot of money very quickly. He stayed on his plantation most of the time, and didn't spend much time in Port-au-Prince society. There were rumors about him—rumors that he was somehow mixed up with magic. No one knew anything for sure.

Toussel didn't really have a bad reputation. So when he told Camille's family that he wished to marry her, they were delighted. Camille herself was not displeased. True, he was a good deal older than she was. But he was still a handsome-looking man, and a very vigorous one. Though he had little in the way of formal education, he was a very intelligent man.

The only thing Camille regretted about marrying Toussel was that she would have to go off and live on his plantation. She knew that she would miss the social life of Port-au-Prince. But she also knew she would be the mistress of a fine, large house.

For a few months life seemed to go well for Camille. She lived on Toussel's plantation. She also came down to Port-au-Prince regularly for parties. She was able to lend her father money. And she had the money to send her younger brother away to school.

Slowly, however, Camille seemed to change. No one could quite be sure what was different. Camille never complained. She never said a

A street in Port-au-Prince

word against her husband. Yet she looked and acted as if she were unhappy. The once lively and talkative girl had become sad and quiet.

Her family tried to talk to her, but she kept saying that everything was fine, that she was perfectly happy. Finally she did speak frankly to her mother. She had no real complaint against Toussel. He was as kind and considerate to her as he always had been. But more and more he seemed to have something else on his mind. Then there were nights when he would ride off early in the evening and not return until dawn. He never explained where he was going and Camille never asked. It was all very strange. It worried and frightened Camille. That was why she seemed so sad.

Her mother asked Camille if she thought Toussel was seeing another woman. Camille said she was quite sure he was not. Her mother than said that perhaps he was having business troubles. Men often acted strangely when they had business troubles. Her mother told Camille that she should not worry. Things would soon come right again. Camille agreed that they probably would.

Their first wedding anniversary was coming up. Camille felt sure that her husband would mark the occasion in some special way. But he said nothing about it. Early in the evening he rode off. Camille was heartbroken. She went to bed and cried herself to sleep.

Near midnight she was awakened. Her husband was standing by her bedside holding a lamp. He was not dressed in his riding clothes. He was dressed in formal evening clothes—as if he were going to a fancy party.

"Put on your wedding dress, and make yourself pretty," he said. "We are going to a party."

Though still half-asleep, Camille was delighted. She thought that her husband had planned an anniversary surprise for her. She assumed her husband was taking her to some late supper dance at a seaside club.

When she joined him on the verandah she asked, "Where is the car?"

"We don't need a car," he replied. "The party is to be there." He pointed to one of the outbuildings. It was one he often used as his office. From it came soft flickering candlelight. Toussel took Camille by the hand and led her to the building. The inside had been decorated like a fancy dining room. In the center of the room was an elegantly set table. Around the table sat four men in evening clothes. There were also two empty chairs. The men did not get up when Toussel and Camille entered. They sat slumped in their chairs. They had wineglasses in front of them, and Camille assumed that they already had too much to drink.

Toussel led his wife to an empty chair. He stood by the other one and began to speak in a strange and confused way:

"Around the table sat four men in evening clothes."

"I beg you . . . Forgive my guests . . . They may seem rude . . . But it is a long time since they tasted wine . . . a long time since they sat at a table . . . but shortly they will drink with you . . . They will raise their arms . . . as I raise mine . . . They will clink glasses with you . . . they will arise . . . they will dance with you . . ."

A feeling of horror crept over Camille. She looked at one of the guests. His fingers were rigidly clasped around the stem of a wineglass. He was not just drunk. She took a candle and held it close to his face. The man was dead. She was sitting at a table with four propped-up corpses.

She screamed and rushed for the door. Toussel tried to stop her, but she was much too fast for him.

The next morning women in a nearby village found her in the marketplace. She was unconscious. When she revived she was completely hysterical. She told her story in a confused way. At first no one believed her. They went to Toussel's plantation. They found the little building. Inside it was all set up for a formal dinner, just as Camille said it had been. But the four "guests" were gone. So was Matthieu Toussel. He was never again seen on his plantation, or indeed anywhere else in Haiti. He was rumored to have fled to some other island. But no one

63

was sure. The police did not try to chase him. What could he be charged with?

Camille never recovered from her experience. She finally became totally insane and spent the rest of her days in a hospital.

Had she always been insane? Had the whole story just been the fantasy of her mind? And if that were the case, why did Toussel run away? And who set up the dinner table, and why?

If the story was true, what had Toussel been planning? What would have happened to Camille if she had not been able to escape?

William Seabrook says he asked that question many times. But he never got a convincing answer. He never even got a convincing theory. Most people would just shrug.

Perhaps it is best that we don't know.

Seabrook told an even stranger story. It was about a magician named Ti Joseph. This magician had created a large number of zombies from corpses he had stolen. He used his magical powers to make the corpses move. Then he hired them out to work in the sugarcane fields. Naturally, Ti Joseph collected all their wages.

One day Ti Joseph had to go off for a few days. He left his wife in charge of the zombies. He told her that they were, on no account, to be given any salt. As soon as a zombie tastes salt, it will become conscious again. Then the zombie will realize that it is a walking corpse.

Joseph was gone longer than expected. His wife was bored just sitting around watching the zombies. There was a carnival in a nearby village. She wanted to go and hear the music, and see the people in their costumes. But she knew she couldn't leave the zombies unattended. So she decided to take them along.

She knew that all the zombies had come from a distant village. Therefore, there was no chance of any of the zombies being recognized by relatives who had recently buried them.

The wife, followed by a line of silent, obedient zombies, went down to the village for the carnival. She sat them down in the town square. All the gayly costumed carnival-goers swirled around them. But the expression of the zombies never changed.

Now this woman was not a hard-hearted person. She was distressed to see that the zombies were not enjoying themselves. She wanted to do something to cheer them up. A woman came by selling candy made from cane sugar and nuts. She thought that it would do no harm to give some candy to the zombies. What she did not know was that the nuts had been well salted.

As soon as the zombies began to eat the candy, and tasted the salt, they changed. They began uttering horrible cries. They then got up and walked straight out of the marketplace and out of the town. They were heading directly toward the village, and the graveyard from which their bodies had been stolen.

As the zombies passed through their hometown, many of the villagers recognized their dead relatives. They guessed what had happened to them. They tried to speak to them. But the zombies would not answer. They would not even turn their heads. They went directly to the graveyard.

Then each zombie threw himself on the grave from which he had been stolen. They tried to dig their way back into the ground with their rotting bony fingers. Finally, they collapsed, completely lifeless again. Then their relatives tearfully restored the bodies to their proper graves.

8

Russia's Walking Corpses

The Russians, like everyone else, fear the dead. But it isn't the spirit of the dead that they fear as much as the corpse itself. The folklore of the Russian peasants is filled with tales of corpses that simply refused to stay put. Sometimes these corpses behaved very much like the creatures that we call vampires.

Here are three old Russian tales which illustrate the point.

A peasant was driving his cart past a graveyard one night. A stranger wearing a red shirt came running up to him.

"Stop, please, and give me a ride."

The peasant said, "Pray take a seat."

The pair drove into the village, and up to the gate of a house. The gate stood wide open. Yet the stranger insisted it was "shut tight." A cross had been painted on the gate. The same thing occurred at several other houses. At the last house in the village the gate was barred. A huge lock hung from it. But there was no cross.

"Wide open," said the stranger in the red shirt.

Suddenly the lock fell to the ground and the gate swung open by itself.

Inside they found two people asleep, an old man and a young boy. The stranger took a pail and put it near the boy. He hit the boy on the back. Immediately blood flowed from his back into the pail. The stranger then drank the pailful of blood. He repeated the same procedure with the old man. Then he said to the peasant, "It is beginning to grow light. Let's go back to my home."

In an instant they were back in the graveyard. The corpse would probably have killed the peasant as well, but a rooster began to crow. Dawn was breaking. The corpse suddenly disappeared.

Later that morning when people went to find the old man and the boy, they discovered both were dead.

Around the year 1800 there was a very powerful governor of one of the Russian provinces. He was a cruel and brutal man. But he had almost total power in his province. The governor was about sixty when he fell in love with a young girl. She was the daughter of one of the minor officials in his government. The girl was already engaged to be married to a young man. This meant nothing to the governor. He ordered the girl's father to have the engagement broken off. Then the father was told that he must consent to a marriage between his daughter and the governor.

The father objected. It did no good. He was told that if he did not agree, he would no longer have a job. There was nothing he could do. The girl, who had to obey her father, was also powerless.

The governor turned out to be every bit as terrible a husband as one might imagine. Most of all, he was insanely jealous of his young wife. He kept her locked in her room much of the time. She could not see anyone unless he was around.

But he was an old man. Soon he became very ill, and was about to die. Even the approach of his own death did not change the governor's evil ways. He called his wife to him and made her swear that she would never marry again. If she did, he told her, he would come back from the grave and kill her. When the evil old man finally died, he was buried in a cemetery across the river from the mansion in which he had lived.

For a while the young widow worried about the threats and the promise she had made. Time passed and nothing happened. Her terrible husband seemed truly, and completely, dead. So her thoughts turned to the young man she had been forced to give up. He had been waiting for the opportunity to marry her. And when he asked, she accepted.

On the night of the engagement feast, horrible cries and shrieks were heard in the old mansion. They came from the young widow's room. The doors were all locked, and it was very hard to break one open. Inside, the servants found that the girl had fainted. Her body was covered with black-and-blue marks.

When she recovered she said that she had gone right to bed after the feast. Then suddenly the dead governor entered the room. He looked exactly as he had in life, except that now he was terribly pale. He yelled at her for breaking her promise and planning to remarry. Then he beat and pinched her until she fainted.

At first no one believed the girl's story. Then a guard at the bridge across the river supported it. The guard said that just before midnight a black coach had driven furiously over the bridge. The coach was supposed to stop, so that the guard could see who was inside. This coach didn't even slow down. The guard was brushed aside.

The new governor didn't really believe the story. But as a precaution he put extra guards at the bridge. The same thing happened, night after night. The guards insisted that the toll barrier would rise by itself when the phantom coach approached.

The phantom coach rumbled over the bridge.

The coach would rumble into the courtyard. As it did, everyone in the old mansion would be overcome by sleepiness. The next morning the young widow would be found in her bedroom bruised and beaten.

The town's physicians could find no explanation. A priest was sent for, to sit by the poor woman during the night. But he too fell asleep, and could not protect her.

People in the town were beginning to grow very frightened. The governor knew that he would have to do something. He stationed fifty cossacks along the bridge. They had orders to stop the carriage at all costs. Promptly, at the usual hour, the carriage could be seen approaching from the direction of the cemetery. The officer of the guard and a priest stood in front of the toll barrier. As the coach approached they said together, "In the name of God and the Czar, who goes there?"

From out of the carriage window came the horribly pale, but quite recognizable, face of the dead governor. "You know very well who I am. Now let me pass."

At that moment the officer, the cossacks, and the priest were thrown back by a mysterious force. The toll barrier went up and the coach rumbled into the old mansion's courtyard. The dead man again tormented his widow. She was very nearly dead herself from all the mistreatment.

The archbishop was now called. He realized that he would have to take the most drastic of measures. He ordered that the governor's corpse be dug up. Then a stake was driven through its heart, and the corpse was reburied.

After that, there was no more trouble from it.

Not all of the Russian walking corpse stories are quite so grim. There is the little tale of the soldier who found himself walking home through a graveyard one night.

Suddenly he heard someone, or something,

"The chapel was empty except for another corpse."

running after him shouting, "Stop! You can't escape me."

The soldier turned around. To his horror, he saw a corpse bearing down on him. The thing was gnashing its teeth. The soldier started to run, but he knew that he couldn't outrun the corpse. So he began looking around for a place to hide. He spied a small chapel and ducked inside.

The chapel was empty except for another corpse that was laid out on a table with candles burning in front of it.

The soldier hid in a corner. Soon the first corpse came dashing into the chapel. The second corpse sprang up and shouted, "What have you come here for?"

"I've chased a soldier in here, and I'm going to eat him."

"Come now, brother. He's run into my house and I'm going to eat him myself."

The two corpses argued. Then they began to fight. The fight continued until dawn. And when the first rays of the sun came through the chapel window, both corpses fell down properly lifeless. The soldier continued his trip home.

9

THE FATE OF GEORGE WOODFALL

This is one of the most famous ghost stories to come out of Australia.

During the 1880s George Woodfall was a rich and respected citizen of the city of Sydney. One day he vanished suddenly, and without a trace. His disappearance caused a sensation. There were all sorts of rumors. But no reason for his disappearance could be found. And there was not a clue as to where he had gone or what had happened to him.

Several years after Woodfall's disappearance the mystery was solved by Rev. Charles Power, and an engineer named William Rowley. Their solution, however, left even a greater mystery. Here is what happened:

Power and Rowley had gone camping in the mountains of the Great Dividing Range. One night they set up their camp in a very remote valley. It was a place where few others had ever gone. Near the camp was a large waterfall. The water poured from the top of a cliff and fell forty feet into the river below.

The first evening Power and Rowley had just finished supper when they saw the sky grow very dark. Suddenly a violent storm burst over them. It was the worst storm either man had ever seen. They ran for cover in a clump of trees.

The furious storm died out almost as suddenly as it had started. There were just a few flashes of lightning left. Power and Rowley were ready to go back and repair their camp. Then they noticed a glow near the top of the waterfall. As they watched—horrified—they saw the glow take the shape of a man. But what a man! It was the figure of someone who had been dead for years. The flesh had shrunk and dried in some parts. In other parts it had rotted away completely. The thing waved its arms, and fell to its knees. Rowley was so frightened he hid his face in his hands. When he looked up again the figure was gone.

He turned to Power, but found the poor man had fainted. When Power woke up he said, "Rowley, I have just had the strangest and most terrifying dream."

Rowley cut him off. "It was no dream. I saw it too."

Power thought for a moment and then said, "That thing would not have appeared to us without some good reason. What do you think it could be?"

"I have no idea," said Rowley. "We'll go up there and find out."

"Good," said Power, "let's go."

"What, now? I thought we should wait until morning. What harm can there be in a little delay?"

Power smiled faintly. "Could you sleep while there was a possibility of that horrible thing appearing again?"

Rowley agreed. So the two men started up the cliff. It proved to be a very difficult climb. Behind the waterfall they could see the entrance to a cave. But there seemed no way to reach that entrance. The two men decided there might be another way into the cave from the top of the cliff.

When they got to the top they found some markings on a tree. Others had been at this spot before. Perhaps the marks were meant to show the cave entrance. They poked around until they found a large hole in the ground. Rowley stuck his lantern in the hole and saw that a sort of crude ladder had been built along the side of the hole.

It was an easy and short climb to the floor of the cave. As the two men felt their way forward, they found a bundle of sticks tied together. The bundle was meant to be used as a torch. The

Australian miners off to the diggings

torch was damp, but with some difficulty Rowley managed to get it lit. The torch gave much more light than the small lantern. Power and Rowley saw that they were now in a vast cavern. At one end of the cavern there was a hole. It seemed to have been smashed into the cavern wall with a hammer.

Rowley took the torch and made his way through the hole.

"What's in there?" asked Power.

"Another cavern, not as large as the first. And there's the waterfall. There's nothing here—I can see all around. Let us—oh! Go away quickly. Don't look!"

But it was too late. Power was already at his side. "What is it? What is it?" he said.

Rowley held the torch out in front of him.

"How awful!" said Power.

The torch illuminated an open grave. At one end of the grave were two skeletons. They seemed to be peering over the edge of the grave.

"They're dead enough," said Rowley. "They can't harm us. Let's see what's in the grave."

In the grave there was a third skeleton. And beneath it, something else. It was something that was nearly but not quite a skeleton. It was the half-rotted thing that had been seen earlier in the evening at the waterfall. It was the thing that had made them look for the cave.

Near the side of the grave was a coat. It was falling to pieces, but they could see that it had been made of an expensive material. In one of the pockets was a tin box. On the box was the name, George Woodfall.

"George Woodfall," said Power. "Why, he must have been murdered after all."

Rowley pried open the box and found it contained a note. The note was George Woodfall's confession.

Woodfall wrote that he had come from a good family. While he was still young he lost all his money. He tried to regain his fortune prospecting for gold. He joined up with three other prospectors. They were rough men. They had all committed crimes in their lives, but they treated him well.

After several months of hard labor, Woodfall and his companions had managed to get together a good deal of gold dust and nuggets. Split four ways, the gold would be a nice sum for each man. But if one man could have it all, he would have a small fortune.

George Woodfall decided to make his fortune back all at once by murdering his companions. They were camping in a cave behind a waterfall. One night Woodfall stabbed the first two before they woke up. The third man woke up and tried to defend himself. Woodfall stabbed him any-

Two Australian gold miners

way. The man uttered a loud scream before he died. Woodfall said he would hear that terrible scream until his dying day.

Woodfall dug a shallow grave and put the three bodies in it. Then he took his gold and went to the city of Sydney.

Woodfall lived quietly for a while. He invested his money wisely, and soon became a very rich man. A year passed and he had almost managed to forget about what he had done. Late one September evening he was sitting alone in his home, when he heard that terrible, and unforgettable, scream. He knew at once what it was, and what it meant.

Then came a voice. "George, you are growing forgetful. We have come to remind you. You know what happened a year ago."

Woodfall tried to speak. But he could say nothing. The voice went on. "George, your time has not yet come. Before it does we will teach you to remember. On Thursday it will have been one year. We shall expect you at the cave. You will come, won't you?"

Woodfall could only whisper, "Yes, I will come."

Each year, for twenty years, on the twentieth of September, Woodfall returned to the cave to spend one terrifying night with his dead companions.

Finally, he knew that his own death was at

hand. He wrote out his confession in the hope that it would bring some peace to his tortured soul.

Rowley and Power were badly shaken by what they had read, and what they had seen. But they had one more act to perform.

They buried the remains of the four men in one grave. Power read the burial service over them.

Power believed that he and Rowley had been guided to the cave that night so that they could find Woodfall's confession. They hoped that his soul could now finally find rest.

10

The Hooded Chair

We have all heard of haunted houses. But haunted furniture? It almost sounds funny. But perhaps you wouldn't laugh if you had ever sat down in the hooded chair.

The story comes from Holland. The piece of furniture was a fancy carved chair that was over 300 years old. On top of the chair's back was an odd structure of leather and wood. It curled over the head of the sitter like a giant hood. It is believed that the hood was supposed to protect the sitter from drafts. It would also have been useful in catching and holding heat from a fireplace. In the drafty and cold houses of sixteenth-century Holland you tried to conserve all the heat you could. But no other chair exactly like this one has ever been seen.

No one knows who made it. No one knows who first owned it. It seems to have been moved around a good deal. We first hear of it in

"On top of the chair's back was an odd structure of leather and wood."

the mid-nineteenth century. Then it was in the possession of the Van Nooy family. They owned a very large house on the edge of Rotterdam.

Very soon people sensed that there was something wrong with the chair. They didn't like to sit in it. The chair was taken out of the parlor. It finally wound up in a corner of the entrance hall. That was a place where no one ever sat. There the chair remained, dusty and forgotten, for nearly 100 years. No, that's not quite true. The members of the Van Nooy family had heard of the chair's evil influence. But they were educated people, and not at all superstitious. They didn't pay any attention to the stories. However, they didn't sit in the chair either. After all, you can never be too careful.

The servants were less educated, more superstitious. They took the hooded chair more seriously. They didn't go near it if they could possibly help it. The chair was barely dusted. And of course they never, ever sat in it, and tried to discourage others from doing so.

Over the Christmas vacation in 1931, little Jan Dunker came from his home in the country to visit his cousins, the Van Nooys, in Rotterdam. While wandering around the house, the eight-year-old boy spotted the unusual-looking chair. He had never seen anything like it before.

To him it looked like a sort of throne. Naturally, he sat right down in it. When one of the servants discovered the boy sitting in the chair, she chased him out of it immediately. The incident was reported to the Van Nooys. They brushed it aside. But they did order the boy never, never to sit in that chair again.

The incident was forgotten. The following day Jan was taken with his cousins, Marie and Mauritz Van Nooy, to a movie in the center of Rotterdam. After they left the show, the three children and a servant who went with them were waiting for the family chauffeur to arrive and take them home.

Suddenly a small car seemed to go out of control. It jumped the curb and swerved onto the pavement. Eight-year-old Jan was struck. The other two children and the servant were unhurt. But Jan died of his injuries without ever regaining consciousness.

The Van Nooy family was saddened by the accident. They were intelligent, modern people. They didn't want to blame the chair. But they didn't want it in their house anymore either. So the chair was put up for sale in a Rotterdam antique auction. It was sold to a dealer in Belgium for a good price.

The chair was loaded into a van and sent off to Antwerp, Belgium. Near the frontier there was an accident. The van driver was killed.

Most of the furniture in the van was destroyed. But the strange hooded chair was untouched.

After that the chair changed hands rapidly. Wherever it went there were rumors of death and tragedy. At one point it wound up in an exhibition of sixteenth-century furniture. The hall in which the exhibition was being held caught fire. Two people were killed and others were injured. Many of the exhibits were damaged or destroyed in the blaze. Nothing happened to the hooded chair.

By the time World War II broke out the chair was in a large house in Belgium. When the Nazis conquered Belgium the house was taken over and used as a military headquarters. The German general, Karl von Lyden, was supposed to have been sitting in the hooded chair when he signed the orders which sent over 1,000 German soldiers to their deaths during a campaign in 1944.

After the war the hooded chair disappeared. It wasn't heard of again until 1949. Five men in a remote village on the French-German border died within a day of one another. They were all apparently healthy men in their twenties and thirties. An investigation indicated that they had all died of natural causes. It was just a strange coincidence, said the police. But a lot of local people thought differently. All five of these men had been customers at a local inn. All five had, at one time or another, sat in what had come to be known as the "bad luck chair." It was an old elaborately carved chair with a strange-looking hood over it!

The owner of the inn didn't know anything about the chair. It had been left to him by a relative a few years earlier. He had kept it in his inn where it quickly got a very bad reputation.

After the deaths the innkeeper roped the chair off. No one was allowed to sit in it. It became a local curiosity. People came to look at it, but not to sit in it. In 1955 the inn closed down and all the contents were sold.

The chair was bought by Dr. Albert Segers, a Belgian physician who also had an interest in the psychic and the occult. Dr. Segers invited a number of psychics and mediums to his house to examine the chair. They all said that they could "feel" something very evil around it. One of them said that the chair was the most evil thing he had ever encountered. They all refused to sit in it.

Dr. Segers tried to make a check of the chair's history. He found some old drawings of Napoleon. A couple of them showed Napoleon on the night of June 17, 1815. On that night Napoleon was in a farmhouse in Belgium. He was planning his strategy for a battle that was to be fought the next day. The battle was at a place called Waterloo. In the battle of Waterloo,

The Emperor Napoleon

Napoleon was completely defeated. It was the battle that ended his career.

The drawings show Napoleon making his plans while seated in a curious-looking hooded chair.

11

THE STOLEN LIVER

This gruesome little tale appears to have originated in Italy. It is not for those of you with weak stomachs. If you go ahead and read it anyway, remember that you have been warned.

The story is about a husband and wife. The husband was an overbearing brute. The wife was meek, and not too bright.

It was the husband's custom to close his shop at noon, and to come to his house. There his lunch would be waiting for him. This particular day he brought home a pound of liver that he had bought in the village. The liver had been a bargain.

Since the noon meal was already waiting for him, he told his wife to cook the liver for dinner.

She brought her husband's lunch out to him in the garden. The ravioli was especially good. He finished lunch with a glass or two of wine. He was in an unusually good mood. He was even willing to listen to his wife talk.

The scene of this tale is a small town in Italy.

She talked about the rich old woman who had died in the village yesterday. They had brought her body to the church next door. It seemed that the old woman had outlived all her friends and relatives. No one had come to view the body.

The wife chattered on for a while. Her husband sat there, half listening. Finally he said, "Enough." She stopped talking instantly. He rose from his chair and walked back toward his shop in the village.

As the afternoon wore on, his wife realized that the time had come to prepare dinner, a dinner of liver. She began cooking the liver slowly, with lots of seasoning, just as her husband liked it.

She lifted the lid of the pot and looked. Was the liver done? It certainly looked done. But with liver, one never could be sure. And if there was one thing her husband hated it was under-cooked liver. So she cut off a small piece from the edge and popped it into her mouth. It was delicious. And it was almost done, but not quite. Perhaps it needed a little more salt too.

She salted the liver and tried another little piece. Yes, that was better. Now a bit more flour. She tried another piece. She found she was extremely hungry. She kept taking one little piece after the other, until she had eaten the liver completely.

Suddenly the poor woman was terrified. What would she tell her husband? That the liver he had brought home for his supper had tasted so good she ate it all herself? The man was a brute. Everybody knew that. He had often beaten her when he was displeased. He would certainly be displeased when she told him what had happened to his dinner.

It was then that she thought of the body of the rich widow lying unattended in the church next door. We will pass over what happened during the next two hours. You can guess.

The meal that evening was an excellent one. The husband rose from the table feeling unusually satisfied. He even managed to grunt a few compliments to his wife. The liver was the tenderest and tastiest he had ever eaten.

Later that evening after the couple went to bed the husband was just drifting off to sleep when he heard it—the voice of an old woman. At first he couldn't quite make out what the voice was saying. It sounded like, "My liver, give me back my liver." But what did that mean? Now the voice was louder. Its message was unmistakable. "My liver, give me back my liver." It didn't make any sense to him.

The wife heard the voice too. And she knew exactly what it meant. She broke down and told her husband what had happened. She told him how she had eaten the liver he bought. She then told him how she had gone next door to the church, and removed the liver from the old woman's corpse. And how she had cooked it and served it to him for dinner.

The man wasn't a particularly sensitive individual. The thought of having eaten the old woman's liver did not trouble him greatly. As he remembered, it had been delicious.

But he was a practical fellow. And as a practical fellow he was afraid of ghosts. Ghosts, he knew, could be very dangerous—particularly if you had something that belonged to them. He had not actually stolen the old woman's liver. But he had eaten it, even if he didn't know what it was at the time. He doubted very much if he would be able to explain that nice little difference to an angry ghost. The ghost would probably take its vengeance on him.

He thought for a moment. The only solution was to return the liver. But how, since he had completely devoured it? Perhaps a substitute liver would satisfy the ghost.

He climbed out of bed and went into the kitchen. He got his wife's largest carving knife. It was the very knife she had used to remove the old woman's liver. When he returned to the bedroom, knife in hand, his wife knew exactly what he planned to do and she fainted.

A few minutes later he stole into the church and gave the old woman a new liver to replace the one he had already eaten.

THE RESTLESS DEAD

As he replaced the liver in the corpse, he thought lovingly of his delicious evening meal. What a waste, he said to himself, what a waste.

The ghost of the old woman was apparently satisfied, because she never troubled him again.

Index

INDEX

INDEX

About the Author

DANIEL COHEN is the author of over a hundred books for both young readers and adults, including some titles he has co-authored with his wife, Susan. Among their popular titles are: *Supermonsters; The Greatest Monsters in the World; Real Ghosts; Ghostly Terrors; Science Fiction's Greatest Monsters; The World's Most Famous Ghosts; Rock Video Superstars; Rock Video Superstars II; Strange and Amazing Facts About Star Trek; Wrestling Superstars; Wrestling Superstars II: Young and Famous: Hollywood's Newest Superstars; and The Monsters of Star Trek*—all of which are available in Archway Paperback editions.

A former managing editor of *Science Digest* Magazine, Mr. Cohen was born in Chicago and has a degree in journalism from the University of Illinois. He appears frequently on radio and television and has lectured at colleges and universities throughout the country. He lives with his wife, daughter, one dog, and four cats in Port Jervis, New York.